T0195973

The Adventures of Prince Santosh

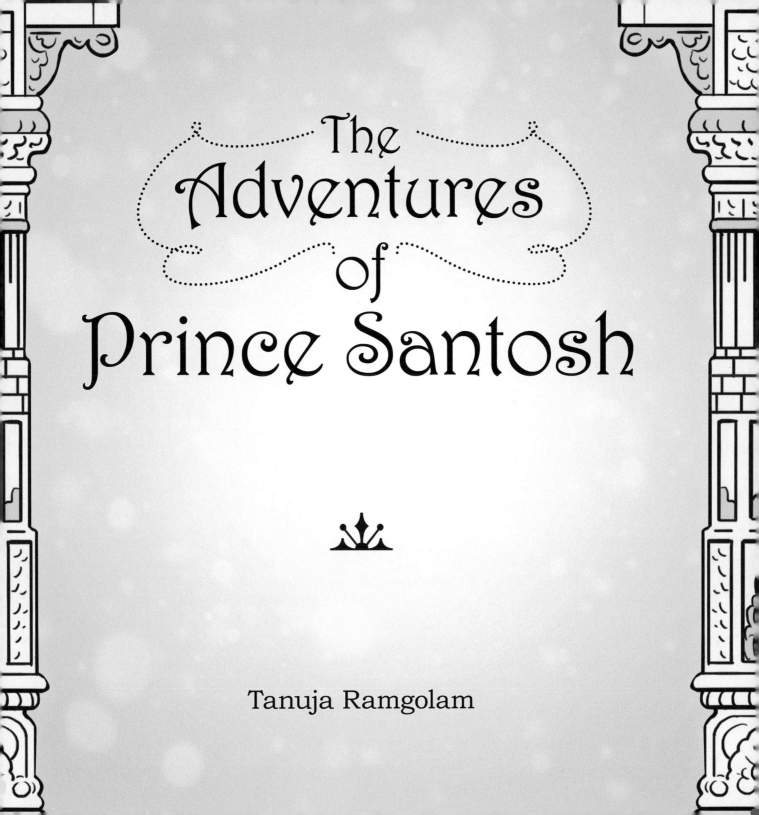

Tanuja Ramgolam

AuthorHouse™ UK
1663 Liberty Drive
Bloomington, IN 47403 USA
www.authorhouse.co.uk
UK TFN: 0800 0148641 (Toll Free inside the UK)
UK Local: 02036 956322 (+44 20 3695 6322 from outside the UK)

This book is printed on acid-free paper.

ISBN: 978-1-6655-9794-4 (sc)
ISBN: 978-1-6655-9795-1 (e)

Print information available on the last page.

Published by AuthorHouse 04/08/2022

authorHOUSE®

Once upon a time, there was a prince name Santosh. He was only six years old but he was very strong. Everyone in the kingdom was scared of him. When Prince Santosh played with his brothers and sisters, he would pull them with such a force their hand would break. Sometimes he would touch them, and they would fall far back and get hurt. For him it was normal, he did not realise his strength. His siblings would complain to the King and Queen. They refused to play with him. The King called Prince Santosh. He gave him a talking to, "Your brothers and sisters can't play with you anymore; I am going to find you some companions to play with. You will have to be careful not to hurt them."

There was no difference in his behaviour. Same thing happened to the other children. "We can't go on like this your Majesty, Prince Santosh has broken hundreds of servant's arms and legs." They protested.

When Prince Santosh was born a Fairy gave him a sabre. "This sabre will protect you and save your life, never let it out of your sight." said the Fairy.

Every time Prince Santosh sharpened his sabre, he became stronger.

Several years passed and Prince Santosh became big and strong. The king was tired of listening to complaints about him. He decided to get rid of Prince Santosh.

One day, the King called Prince Santosh and told him, "There is a big hungry elephant in the garden, everyone is scared of it. As you are my brave son, you go and feed the elephant." One thing the king did not tell Prince Santosh is that the elephant was mad. The King thought the elephant will crush prince Santosh and that would be the end of him.

After a few hours, the King saw Prince Santosh in his room. "You did not feed the elephant as I ordered?" questioned the king.

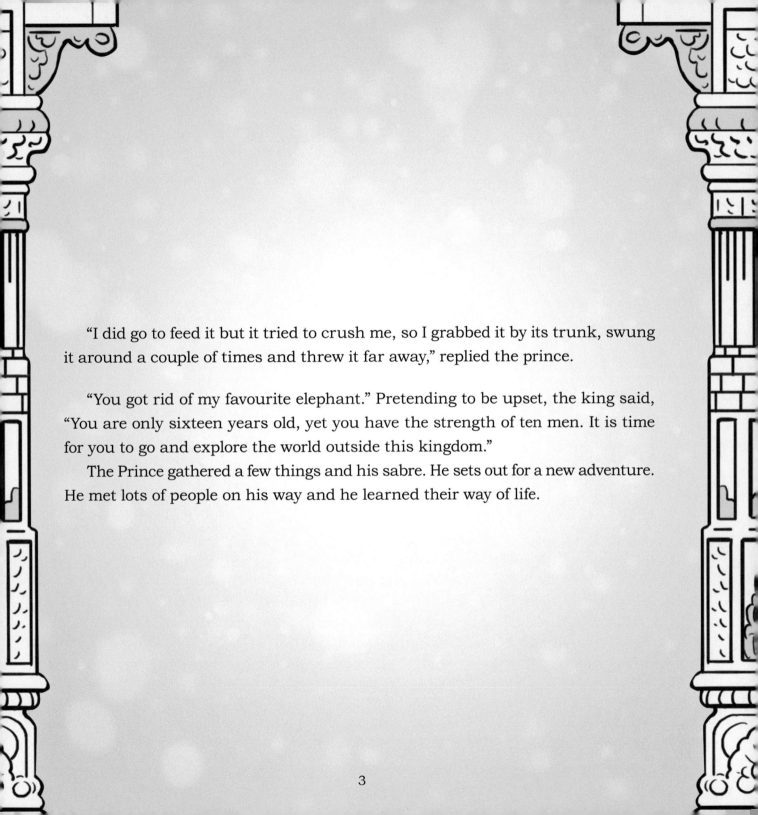

"I did go to feed it but it tried to crush me, so I grabbed it by its trunk, swung it around a couple of times and threw it far away," replied the prince.

"You got rid of my favourite elephant." Pretending to be upset, the king said, "You are only sixteen years old, yet you have the strength of ten men. It is time for you to go and explore the world outside this kingdom."

The Prince gathered a few things and his sabre. He sets out for a new adventure. He met lots of people on his way and he learned their way of life.

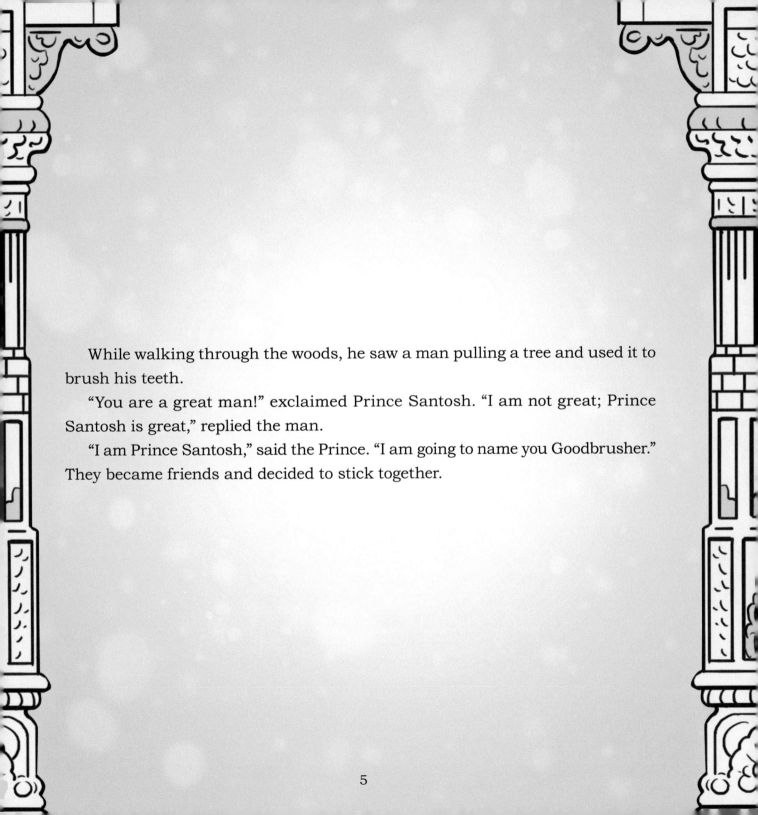

While walking through the woods, he saw a man pulling a tree and used it to brush his teeth.

"You are a great man!" exclaimed Prince Santosh. "I am not great; Prince Santosh is great," replied the man.

"I am Prince Santosh," said the Prince. "I am going to name you Goodbrusher." They became friends and decided to stick together.

On their way, they met a man who had such long and strong moustache. He was using it to fix the bridge that was broken on one side. There were many chariots on both sides waiting to pass.

Prince Santosh said, "You are a great man!"

"I am not great; Prince Santosh is a great man," replied the man.

"I am Prince Santosh and I will name you Bridgeman."

They got together and carried on their journey. They had just gone a couple of miles when they saw a man looking up towards the sky and clapping his hands and smiling.

"What are you looking at and why are you clapping your hands?" asked Prince Santosh.

"I am looking at the angels dancing in the sky," responded the man. Prince Santosh and his friends could not see anything in the sky. "You are a great man!" stated the Prince.

"I am not great," uttered the man "Prince Santosh is great."

"I am Prince Santosh and I am going to name you Goodlooker," declared the Prince.

All four of them went to a village and built a house for themselves to stay. Early morning, they got up and went hunting. In the forest, they saw a man shooting a bird but the bird did not fall. Prince Santosh questioned him, "What happened to the bird? It did not fall."

The man replied, "When I shoot a bird today it would fall the next day."

"You are a great man!" exclaimed the Prince.

"I am not great; Prince Santosh is great," said the man.

"I am Prince Santosh and I will name you Goodshooter."

Now that they were a bigger team, they decided they will take turns to stay home to cook and clean for everyone while the rest go hunting. In the morning, they all got up to go hunting except for Bridgeman who stayed to cook and clean the house.

After finishing his chores, Bridgeman went outside and sat on a rock to have a rest with a cup of tea. When he took a sip, he found a big bad wolf standing next to him. "Give me a match!" ordered the Wolf. Bridgeman put his cup down to check his pocket. The Wolf grabbed Bridgeman's hand. He pulled a whisker from his chin and tied bridgeman hands. "I am going to eat you," said the Wolf. "Please do not eat me, there are lots of nice food that I cooked in the kitchen, you can have all of it," begged Bridgeman. The Wolf took Bridgeman in the kitchen, put a heavy bag of rice on top of him, ate all the freshly cooked food and then left. Bridgeman managed to untie his hands but he could not move the bag of rice.

When Prince Santosh and his friends came back from hunting, they saw the kitchen in a mess and Bridgeman on the floor under a big bag of rice. They asked him what has happened. He told them when he was getting some rice to cook. The bag fell on him. He was ashamed to tell them he was scared of the Wolf.

They helped Bridgeman up and then together they cooked some food to eat. The next day, it was Goodlooker's turn to stay at home. Same thing happened to him. The wolf came, ate all the food and put a big bag of lentils on top of him. Prince Santosh was thinking how is this possible. There must be something they are not telling me. In the morning, he told his friends he is going to stay and cook and clean today. His friends went hunting. On their way to the forest, they told each other what really happened to them. They decided to climb a tall tree to see what Prince Santosh will do when the wolf comes.

After doing all his chores, Prince Santosh went outside and sat on the same rock his friends been sitting.

Just then the wolf came and said, "Do you have a match?", "No" replied the Prince. "Do you have a match?" the wolf asked again. "No, I said, don't you understand!" yelled the Prince. The wolf tried to grab Prince Santosh's hands, without wasting any time Prince Santosh grabbed the Wolf arms and swung him around and around and threw him far away.

The Wolf got up and came back to fight with the prince. Prince Santosh chased the Wolf down a hole. They both fought, then the ground shook and opened up, the Wolf fell down and various rocks fell on him. That was the end of the Wolf.

Prince Santosh's friends who were watching from up the tree came down and followed him to the hole. Inside the hole there was a cave. It went deeper and deeper. The Prince was looking for a way out when he found four beautiful girls locked in a room and there were several chests full of treasures. He unlocked the door, the girls told him there is no way out except through the hole that he came down. They all started shouting, "Help!".

Prince Santosh's friend heard them; they threw a long rope down the hole. The Prince tied one girl and a treasure chest and sent them up. Bridgeman who was first in the line took the girl and said, "She is mine." The Prince sent the next three girls and the treasure chests. One after the other, his friends took one girl each and left the treasures. When it was time to pull the Prince up, the rope came down. His friends were busy with the girls.

"How am I going to get out now?" thought the Prince. Just then a Toad came along.

"What are you doing here?" asked the Toad, "The Wolf will eat you if he finds you here."

The Prince told the Toad what happened to the Wolf and how he got stuck in the cave.

The Toad said to the Prince, "I can help you get out of here, bring me ten gallons of water. After I drink it, you sit on my back and pinched me gently, I will jump, then I will throw you out of the hole." The Prince did exactly as he was told. He pinched the toad aaannnd... nothing happened. The Toad just spilled all the water out.

"What happened?" inquired the Prince.

"You pinched me too hard," replied the Toad.

"Go get some more water," ordered the Toad. Prince Santosh brought some more water for the toad to drink, he then sat on the toad's back. This time he did not pinch him. He just scratched his back gently. The toad jumped so high. He threw the Prince out of the hole.

Seeing the Prince, all of his friends moved away from the girls saying you belong to Prince Santosh.

"My Friends you need to live your own life. Take your girls and a treasure chest. Go start a new life. If ever I find my life in danger you will come and help me, won't you?" requested the Prince. "We will be there straight away, but how would we know when to come?" observed his friends.

"Goodbrusher when you will try to pull a tree to brush your teeth and the tree is too hard to pull, you will know then that I am in trouble. Goodlooker when you look up in the sky you do not see any angels dancing, that's when you know my life is in danger. Goodshooter when you shoot a bird today and it does not fall the next day, you know I am in trouble. Bridgeman when your moustache starts falling, you know I am in trouble. You will need to find my sabre; my life lies in my sabre," clarified the Prince. He told his friends his secret. They parted their separate ways.

A few years passed, the Prince has turned into a handsome, strong young man. He was walking near a river; when from a distance he could see something glittering. When he went closer, he saw a beautiful girl with golden hair sitting on the bank of the river.

He introduced himself and then asked her name. "Anjalina" she said with a smile. They got talking as if they knew each other for a long time. The Prince fell in love with Anjalina instantly. "I am a traveller; I am looking for a place to stay for a few days." He uttered, "You can stay with me if you like, my house is not far from here."

The Prince hesitated. "Won't your parents object to have a stranger in their house," he queried. "I live on my own in a big house. You seem pleasant and it would be nice to have some company," she responded. The Prince followed Anjalina to her house. Every morning the Prince will go hunting and then gather woods for Anjalina to cook their food.

One day, Anjalina went to the river for a swim. Her hair got tangled in a twig. She pulled her hair out but some of her hair got caught and it was stuck on the twig.

Some days later, the twig travelled further down the river. A Prince named Rajveer was having lunch with his friends when he saw something glittering in the water. He picked up the twig with the hair on. "How beautiful would the girl with this golden hair be?" he thought.

Prince Rajveer went home and told his father the king he wants to marry the girl who this hair belongs to, showing the king the golden hair on the twig.

Next day, the King put out a notice, whoever will bring the news about the girl with golden hair will be handsomely rewarded.

An old woman who goes around begging for food knew Anjalina is the girl the King is looking for and she has seen Anjalina with Prince Santosh. I will have to separate them so that Prince Rajveer can marry her and I will get lots of money. (thought the cunning woman)

Without telling anyone what she knows the old woman went to Anjalina's house and beg her for a place to stay. "I will do all your chores in the house," she promised. As Anjalina was a kind hearted girl she agreed to let her stay.

One morning, when Prince Santosh went hunting in the forest the old woman seizes the opportunity to talk to Anjalina. "You like this young man?" she asked her. "Are you going to marry him?"

Feeling a bit shy Anjalina said, "I do like him."

"Then you need to know all about him. He shouldn't keep any secrets from you."

"I know everything about him," protested Anjalina.

"Do you know in what his life lies? If something happens to him one day, you can help him," snooped the old woman.

Anjalina started thinking, "I don't know where his life is kept safe. I will ask him when he comes home tonight."

In the evening when Prince Santosh came, Anjalina asked him if he loves her. "Yes, I do" replied the Prince.

"If you love me, you shouldn't keep any secrets from me," commented Anjalina.

"Yes," nodded the Prince. "Then tell me where is your life hidden?" requested Anjalina. Prince Santosh thought for a minute then said "My life is hidden in that broom." He pointed to a broom in the corner of the room.

Outside their room, the old woman was listening. The next day, after Prince Santosh went hunting the old woman took the broom and went behind the house to burn some leaves she gathered in the garden. Then she put the broom in the fire to burn.

In the evening when the sun went down, Anjalina was waiting for the return of the Prince. The old woman was watching and thinking he is not coming back now, just at that moment Prince Santosh appeared in a distance.

"How is that possible?" thought the old woman. He lied. She waited for Prince Santosh to go to bed, she crept in Anjalina's room and told her, "The Prince has lied to you. How can you marry someone who doesn't trust you with their secrets?"

Anjalina went straight to Prince Santosh's room and asked him why he lied to her. Prince Santosh reassured her of his love for her and finally told her his life is hidden in his sabre. At night when they were sleeping the old woman stole the Prince's sabre and burnt it. She ran to the King's palace to tell him where Anjalina lives and to collect her rewards.

Prince Santosh woke up with pain in his body. He staggered in the room. He knocked a jug of water. Anjalina heard the noise, she came running. "What happened?" she asked. She was scared and she started crying. "I don't think I will survive, if anything happens to me don't bury me, put me in a glass casket my friends will find me," saying that the Prince collapsed in her arms.

In the garden, Anjalina put Prince Santosh's body in a glass casket. She went to the river where she met him for the first time and cried her heart out.

Suddenly, some soldiers came and took Anjalina with them.

Early in the morning, Goodbrusher was trying to pull a tree to brush his teeth but unfortunately, he could not. The tree would not budge. He went to his wife and said to her I have to leave; my friend is in trouble. "I will come with you," said his wife.

On the other side of the village, Goodshooter was looking for the bird he shot yesterday, it was nowhere to be found. He thought of Prince Santosh, something must have happened to him. He went home and told his wife "I must leave my friend is in trouble."

"I will come with you to help," said his wife.

When Goodlooker looked up in the sky, he could not see any angels dancing. He told his wife he needed to go and help Prince Santosh. His wife also accompanied him.

Bridgeman's moustaches started falling. He realised Prince Santosh needs his help. He went in search of the Prince with his wife besides him. They all met at the same place where they were separated. They all said the same thing together "Prince Santosh's life is in danger."

They followed the path the Prince took last time they saw him. On their way, they asked a passer-by if he knows where Prince Santosh lived. The man said he has never heard of this name before, but when they described him as the tall, strong man with big muscle, black curly hair and fair complexion. He remembered seeing him with Anjalina. He guided them to her house and left.

The place was deserted. They searched everywhere, but there was no sign of anyone. When they went at the back of the house, they found his sabre. "He must be around here somewhere," they said at once. Then they went to the garden where they found Prince Santosh lying in a glass casket. "We must sharpen his sabre." stated Goodshooter. They lifted the glass cover off and took turn to sharpen the sabre.

Once the sabre started shining, Prince Santosh regained consciousness and opened his eyes. His friends were pleased to see him alive. When Prince Santosh did not see Anjalina among them, he asked them if they have seen her.

"There wasn't anyone here when we came," answered his friends. They all started looking for Anjalina. They came to a village asking everyone about Anjalina. A man who works in the palace told them that she is getting married to Prince Rajveer in two days.

"My wife told me she is getting married against her will. She doesn't look happy," explained the man.

"Because she loves me," mumbled Prince Santosh. "We need to get her out of there," he shouted.

How can we get inside the palace? There would be hundreds of soldiers around they said to one another? "There is a way, the King is having a ball tonight," said the man. "My wife is going to get Anjalina ready for the wedding, she can take some of the ladies with her to help her escape, and I am going to be one of the cooks, the men can come with me as helpers."

Prince Santosh and his friends managed to enter the palace in disguise. Once inside Prince Santosh sneaked upstairs to Anjalina's room. She was ecstatic to see him. "You are alive, I am so happy to see you." They embraced, in between tears she said, "Take me away from here." His friend's wives took Anjalina to the balcony where Bridgeman was waiting below, he threw his long moustache to the ladies. They tied it to the balcony and went down using it as a rope.

At that very moment, Prince Rajveer came to check on Anjalina. He drew his sword out and fought with Prince Santosh. Anjalina and the ladies went down, Prince Santosh pushed Rajveer out of the way. He cut the moustache off the balcony and jumped off.

Prince Rajveer followed him. Prince Santosh's friends came to help him. They fought with the soldiers.

Prince Santosh fought with Prince Rajveer with one hand and with the other hand he pushed the soldiers on the ground. Goodbrusher pulled some trees and threw them on the soldiers.

They got into a chariot which Goodlooker was driving. They left the palace far away. In the dark night, they could not see where they were going.

Finally, the chariot stopped. They found themselves in front of an old temple in the middle of a forest. Prince Santosh's friends told him, there is no better time than this to get married. They woke up the priest and had Prince Santosh and Anjalina married. Prince Santosh thanked his friends for their help.

Dawn broke out. Everyone was happy. Prince Santosh's friends said their good byes and went to their own home. Prince Santosh and Anjalina went back to their home.

The End.

Printed in the United States
by Baker & Taylor Publisher Services